NONE
SHALL
SLEEP

Otep Shamaya

NONE
SHALL
SLEEP

Written by Otep Shamaya

Centaurs Breed Publishing

NONE

SHALL

SLEEP

Written by Otep Shamaya
Cover design by Joey James
Artworxofjoeyjames@facebook.com

Centaurs Breed Publishing

For information about this publication contact:
you@artsaves.me or online at www.artsaves.me

This is a work of fiction. Names, characters, places, and incidents, are either the product of the author's imagination or are used fictitiously. And any resemblance to actual persons, living or dead, business establishments, events, or locales is entirely coincidental.

Unending gratitude and love to my friends, my family, and to you dedicated reader, for allowing me inside your mind.

Table of Contents

Now that I'm awake,
none shall sleep.

MINE

I have been here for hours, watching, waiting, coiled in the void of this moonless night. I arrived early just so I could prolong the sensation, to savor every breath, every tickle of anticipation. And right on time *there she is.* My beloved.

I can hear the metallic click clacking of her cheap stilettos long before I can see her. The echo ricochets through the concrete canyon of brownstones now darkened with sleep. Her shadow angles in, long and lean, slicing the paddocks of light emanating from the aged streetlamps lining the frozen walk.

And there's my girl. Arms crossed, walking briskly, swells of smoky breath billowing from beneath a flannel scarf that she has wrapped around her nose and mouth and twists around her neck and shoulders. Oh, but those eyes. I can't stop staring at those deep deer-brown eyes and spider leg eyelashes. She keeps her hands snug deep in the pockets of her thick overcoat and has tied her long copper hair back neatly into a tight bun. Everything is perfect.

I already know the shortcut she takes from the bus stop to her building. I already know how many steps she ascends before reaching her front door. I know she fumbles through her purse and chooses the wrong key every... single... night. *I know she lives alone.*

I know how many seconds I will wait once she steps inside, once the lock clicks and she believes she is secure and out of harm's way. I know how long I've wanted her. I know this is worth the wait.

She passes my position without notice. Her thoughts are far, far away from us. But mine are right here, with her, in the singing spiral of the moment. I don't notice it right away but my brow is dotted with sweat. My mouth has begun watering and I begin to sense a dizzying hum clotting behind my eyes and it summons my soul to stillness. It must be her buoyant silhouette and the rhythmic pricking of those tacky heels that coagulate and bewitch me.

I think about those shoes, so tawdry. I don't know why she chooses to ruin this moment by wearing them. You can tell a lot about these carrion people by what they put on their feet: who they think they are, what they wish they were, what they want out of life…this one wishes to be noticed. *Wish granted.*

The clacking has faded. She has walked four blocks since I first spotted her and is just about home. The moment is swelling. I feel like a god staring at the edge of my creation. This is the glint of the sword in the firelight, the tip of the spear as it enters flesh. It's time I make her mine.

The soft sound of snow crunching underfoot gives me comfort. I adore this time of year. The silence of the night engulfs me. The inky murk of November has rolled over the crooked dome of the boney sky. The hive world slows in the frost of a taunting season. Winter is late but welcome. The cold silence amplifies everything: the icy air, the barren sky, the slow heavy thump of my hollow heart.

Her building is at the end of the block. She lives on the north side. Bottom floor. Middle apartment. I see her. It happens just as I said it would. 1-2-3-5 steps. Wrong key. Lock clicks. She drops her coat and scarf in the entry and kicks off those vexing shoes. She shuffles to the kitchen and pours a glass of scotch. *(I am inside)* She lights a cigarette and blows the smoke over the match. *(She doesn't notice)* She sucks the end of her tobacco killing stick in long, steady drags, exhaling slowly, controlling release. The gray smog rises from her lips like a cremation furnace. The simple elegance of this quiet moment is almost irresistible. *(But, I wait)*

She slugs back the scotch, finishes her smoke and ashes it in the sink. She unties her hair and enters the hallway, past the childless bedroom with the empty crib, past the tiny altar coated in wax like a wedding cake, and into the bathroom where she undresses and stands nude staring into a mirror, tugging at the tiny creases around her eyes and mouth, checking her profile, pulling at her saggy belly and looking defeated.

The years have not been kind.

She sighs and starts a bath, *(I wait)* humming as she pours perfumed oil in the water. It spreads out like a lavender phantom over the aged porcelain. *I savor every second of this.*

No one will ever know her the way I have. When people are alone, when they've removed the cultural costumes and facades, they reveal who they really are. No, this moment, whether she knows it or not, is just for us.

Bubbles billow up and crowd the tub. She sits on the edge of the bath. (I wait) Her naked body folds in half, tits hanging like mushy stalactites over her lap. *Oh, precious.* She closes her eyes and holds her head as if it might float away. *(And I wait)*

For a moment, my thoughts drift again, this time to the hammer I am holding. The handle is smooth as bone, the forged steel head is heavy, and I feel powerful. She reaches for the faucet and I snap back to the moment. Bubbles brim the edge of the tub. Her fingers check the water temperature and I'm ready.

I move behind her.

She doesn't hear.

I swing the hammer.

She doesn't see.

I crack her skull.

She's in the tub. Facedown.

I'm drowning her.

Mashing her head to the bottom, knifing the claw of the hammer into her spine and ribs over and over and over and over and over and over and over and over and over and over and over and over.

Her body stops pretending to care and surrenders as it's supposed to. Just to be sure, I press hard, keeping her head beneath the bloody water a few moments more. Her neck snaps, her nose breaks, and her face collapses against the bottom of the tub.

She's pissed herself in the struggle. I'm covered in gore and soapy water. I see my face in the mirror and foam has formed a half smile over the black nylon I'm wearing.

I lean to her.

The water glistens like glass.

I hover over the surface; soft breath causing tiny quakes, and whisper, "I have done to you what nature has done to me."

She doesn't reply.

I make a mental note to grab the shoes on my way out so I can burn them. I use wire cutters to snap off her ring finger. A keepsake. But I don't want to leave. Not yet. I lean over and turn off the light.

The house is dark and quiet. Empty.

Just like I am now.

NONE SHALL SLEEP

There are nights so vacant
and hushed, I can feel the texture of my tattered
soul moving within me. Black tar. Dripping,
sticky, and thick. A soft, slow secretion of
indifference slopping through the hollow suit I
use as a body.

Heads, eyes, ears, fingers and limbs.
Trophies that once thrilled and delighted now
gather dust and fade from memory. The world

has grown heavy. I feel numb and uninspired.

Perhaps this is why I choose to write this now, to incite my spirit in the fear of being exposed, the fear of being forgotten, the fear of losing all meaning in my work to the lies and hysterics that plague the scope of my labor.

Have you heard what they say about me? Have you seen the things they've written? Nothing but vulgar twaddle disgorged from the minds and mouths of the mentally deficient. I suppose it shouldn't vex me that these meat creatures (my *meatures*, if you will) are so shallow and cruel. But it does. I don't know why they can't recognize the tremendous gift I'm giving them and their rodent kind. But until I sanitize the specious claims spat by the depraved beasts that breed like bacteria in the sewers and swamps of your society I will remain paralytic and stolid. And what kind of life is this without passion? *No life at all.*

You see I need those beautiful moments when I'm unyoking my opponent, limb from limb, in the knotted irons of combat. I need to feel the burning acid of death boiling through my veins, our bodies crushing and colliding, taught and tender. This violent emotional intercourse is the closest thing to true intimacy that I can ever hope to achieve. My flesh against theirs, bone on bone, tightened sinews, labored breath, wreathing in the grisly trough of chaos, then everything collapses and with a breath, I am rapt in the bloody jaws of climax, siphoning the life out of my enemy, expanding as they diminish. And then, it disperses. And I find myself destroyed and reborn in the terrifying tranquility of hiatus.

Such is the twisted, sadistic, cyclical life of a murder junkie.

Clinically, I would be classified as a "violent sociopath with severe psychosis". Serial killer. Mass murderer. Monster. Devil. Labels, labels, labels. They are what they are. But I don't possess the emotional architecture to be anything other than I am. I thrive because I embrace this evil for what it is: a gift.

Most of what is written here will be difficult for the common mind to digest. So if unfiltered honesty offends you stop reading immediately. It won't be a delicate retelling. This isn't for emotional amateurs. I've been serving active combat duty for quite a time now, and whatever luck I may have had has long since run out. So, I need to do this now before it's too late.

My motivations are simple and selfish. I'm compelled to leave a lucid recollection of how I came to this feral fate and erase the fabrications, exaggerations, and silly superstitions excreted by the insects of your race.

I detest those secret circles that celebrate the madness and malice of my bloody rancor. The self-proclaimed "Suicide Society" is the worst. Ego-driven hipster rodents fashioning blogs and social networks beseeching me to end them so their lives can taste some sliver of celebrity. These moral pygmies purposely degrade the sanctity of my craft for their lowly amusement. Well, let it be known here and now that I fervently repudiate their desires and stand as stone in opposition to oblige them. Truth is, *it isn't any fun if they want it.*

And I know of the droves of misguided souls claiming I was created by a clandestine government agency to keep the yokels in line. This, of course, is complete nonsense. Stupidity is an anthropophagite disease. I have no political affiliation and I'm nobody's pawn. But alas, these conspiracy nuts aren't nearly as agitating as the wretched zealots who revere me as a mystic or messiah.

In the muddled minds of these silly sycophants, I was once an armor plated, gold emblazoned, multi-headed death god, speaking in tongues and splitting the sky with fire sent back in the form of a coagulated fiend to redeem the world of wickedness. Actually, that doesn't sound so bad. But I digress. It seems this era suffers from a fly-infested famine of common sense.

I often wonder why any of us deserve to exist if we allow this kind of ethical violence to continue. Yes, very Spartan of me, I know. But theirs is a mutant-voodoo-extremist-creed that has spawned one too many amateur copycats and these counterfeit killers lack imagination. Their work is sloppy and uninspired. It's embarrassing.

So allow me to be clear, I'm not a god, I'm not a hero, I don't deserve worship or respect.

What I warrant is fear.

For I'm a fiend, dear reader, the filth of humanity, breast-fed from devils, and now, I eat my own kind.

COAGULANT

I used to dream of being inside
the womb, fetal universe, black holes and
emptiness, orbiting the massive planet of my
mother's booming heart.

Tiny yolk-body tethered like an
astronaut, adrift in the tranquil spume of
desolate bliss. *Tabula rasa.* Fungi fingers
inching from chubby stems, reaching for that
great thumping-whoosh of muscle, blood and

power that wobbled like a snarling god above me.

Each beat of her horrible heart would push, as if swallowing, a molten lead life-force that aerated and transmuted me from corpulent larva to fledgling killer to the exemplary destroyer I've become. My body would pop and grow as if being inflated by phantoms.

There is always this distressing hiss like glass burning then suddenly I would detonate, fully grown, from my mother's belly into a barbwire bramble where my flesh would rip and shred to bloody confetti. And as the debris settled, I would be reduced to a gelatinous membrane retching and drying on the cold floor of some forgotten tomb.

My fibrous head, translucent as a bell jar, rolling slowly, side to side, would search deep into the godless black with great staring eyes for a light, for a sign, for anything other than indifference. The universe would never oblige.

I would always wake lashing out, trembling and gasping for air as if I was drowning. I haven't had that dream in a while. Though, to be honest, as grim and unpleasant as it was, I do miss it. I don't know why.

Perhaps it's the inert serenity of embryonic nothingness that I secretly desire. *Ignorant and empty, blissful in the void.*

Perhaps it's the monopoly this dream seems to possess over my emotional response systems. Perhaps I just enjoy the trip.

But you're not here to read about dreams or serenity, or be my *the-rapist*, are you? No. You want chaos.

You want my awful reality to free you from the anchors of your own private decay. Yes? You want to know the story? So be it. Let's not stray.

But fair warning. This a strange and savage odyssey, both precarious and plentiful as it billows through a polytrophic universe freckled with a spattering stratum of wormholes and quantum portals that open to an infinite multiplicity of exotic locales in diamond studded sewage systems and twisted, sadistic feral dimensions. Sort of.

My early life was a lecherous amalgam of perversity, broken bones, isolation, leather belts and cigarette burns.

There is no secret to uncover. I'm the sum of my parts.

My conception was feral and unsympathetic.

IN THE BEGINNING

I was born on a Tuesday.

No magi, no navigational star, no angels singing hymns to my arrival. It was ugly and unembellished. I was a premature, nicotine, alcohol, cocaine, and opiate addicted, three-pound ball of chaos spawned from the most traditional of all unions, a conflicted couple of unwed teens.

To be clear, this isn't a love story. This isn't a romantic fable from antiquity. My parents (in as much as their mating created my physical self) wern't two star-crossed lovers from opposite sides of the tracks sent to ruin by the powers that be.

No.

They were vulgar and dull and came from a shitty suburb in a shitty city bursting at the seams with a surplus of failures, phonies, and fiends.

Most of what I know about them has been gathered through years of investigation using genealogical records, my mother's scribbled diary, hacked computer files, and a vigorous hallucinogenic trance induced teleportation with the blood-drinking Oracle of Ihped.

We'll get into that much later but for now, *a history lesson.*

I want to sledgehammer the human race
and leave nothing but dust.

GEN ISIS

Cassandra, from the Greek *"she who entangles men"*, was my mother's name. She was very proud of it. She wasn't to be called Cassie, or Sandy, or Sandra, she preferred the full flavor of every fizzling syllable.

Cassandra. The sound serpents make as they coil around each other. Cassandra. The whiff of sulfur as the match head bursts into flame. Cassandra. The shadow carved into my soul.

43

Her mother named her after a Christian martyr from the Middle Ages but Cassandra preferred the pagan version.

And just like the hexed character in Greek mythology, both were beautiful and mad, cursed to know their fate but could do nothing to change it or do anything to persuade anyone to believe it.

On the outside, my Cassandra was a perfect example of high society. A "saucy blonde" (the papers called her) from the right side of the tracks with all the gifts and breaks a rich kid could ever hope to have. But on the inside, her soul was receding into madness.

Her parents were a pair of politically conservative jackasses sewn into the quilt of local aristocracy. They did their best to raise her to be just as sterile and antiseptic and frothing with hypocrisy as they were.

But, Cassandra was a designer-jeans-rebel with an insatiable appetite for self-destruction. She wasn't afraid of anything except being bored.

She was vice-president of the student council, team captain of the tennis team, proconsul for the Metropolitan Junior Achievers, and a blowjob-bartering black tar junkie. *Such sophistication.*

My father, or rather the sperm donor, was called Vincent. He was a self-educated street savage who had been in and out of foster care since he was taken from his mother's shivering arms detoxing in a prison hospital.

Scanning her diary, the only thing my mother ever wrote about him was a fractured poem of sorts, *"Vincent. My dark thorn, butter cream skin, kindness behind his icy sapphire eyes."*

And then on the following page was scribbled "Vince!! FUCKING COLD-HEARTED ASSHOLE" with boiling ferocity. I can only fashion a guess that one of these entries was written while high, the other dopesick.

Vincent's life can be deduced to a series of numbers. He was given to an orphanage after

6 hours of life, he committed his first act of arson at the age of 8 when he set fire to Father Flannigan's garage apartment and was sent to a Juvenile Detention Center for 3 years.

His second act of arson was at age 11, Father Flannigan again, but this time the entire house burned to ash. Cops arrested Vincent but soon discovered Father Flannigan had been taking photos of altar boys in their swim trunks. He was immediately transferred and Vincent was never charged.

Instead, Vincent was passed from foster family to group home to foster family for a few years where he learned to fight, learned to cheat, steal, and the designer art of selling dope.

He started dealing when he was 13, started using when he was 15, and was a certified psycho by the time he was 18.

When he met my mother, he was living with his 7th foster family and 8 other throwaway kids.

He was a selfish, self-sustaining narcissist that enjoyed violence and self-destruction.

Now you see why I like him.

It is important to note that I never met my biological parents but I do *know* them. What I mean is, as sole heir to their cruel house, I do see bits and pieces of them in me (and likewise) but only as vapor.

Indeed, traces of this and that, tempers and certain proclivities, but what I don't and won't ever possess is their eagerness to yield. It just isn't in me.

For better or worse, I am not a quitter.

GOMORRAH NOIR

Cassandra was broke but desperate for a fix. Her normal dealer had been busted for traffic warrants and was sitting out his bid in County.

Her friend recommended Vincent who was known to barter. Cassandra was fine with that. She did what she always did when she was in a bind. She fucked.

She met Vincent in the men's room at the Gas-n-Go and haggled off a round of anal for a used needle and a bag of shitty smack.

They did the deed in the handicap stall with Cassandra's face suspended over the toilet as she prepared her rig.

According to Cassandra's messy diary, Vincent was, forgive me, a *3-pump-chump* (her words), and after just a few punches to the stink-hole, knifed his messy prick into Cassandra's puss and emptied his load inside her.

No condom.
She didn't notice.

He wiped his dick on the rotating towel roll, and left her stabbing her scabs with a charged syringe.

Once she finally found a vein, she injected the death, and collapsed into oblivion completely unaware of the parasitic fetal cells uniting and dividing inside her. And that was the extent of their affair.

I believe she tried for another go with him a few weeks later but I don't believe Vincent was much of a fan. He didn't go back for seconds.

Now, I haven't the words to express just how shameful all of this is for me.

Who could be proud of such a hideous start? I only share this with you because I think it's important to impart just how difficult and dangerous it's been for me.

To show you the obstacles I've overcome and the level of soaring success I've earned with all the odds against me. Thank you for not judging me, gentle reader. I will reward you by continuing the story.

Cassandra continued *smoking-pole* (in the parlance) for dope and pretending to be a perfect example of *haut monde* while I coalesced inside her slagheap uterus.

Meanwhile, Vincent decided to liberate himself from this mortal coil in a blaze of glory.

I AM BECOME DEATH,
THE DESTROYER OF WORLDS

Medical experts dismissed

it as drug driven dementia, the bible beaters
said it was demonic possession, and the salon
society chattered night and day about a sordid
lovers triangle that made their gossip-hungry
eyes beam with delight.

*Gossip, gossip, gossip, the cheap
confection for a feeble mind.*

These over-processed, over-painted, overweight hens clucked on and on beneath their rotten breath that my father might've been exploring the life of a secret sodomite with a male teacher or perhaps another student.

I make no judgments here, but what bothers me most is how much it bothered them. Who are they to judge anyone when they are so weak and deficient?

Perhaps if they had spent a little less time judging others and focused on their own lives, Vincent wouldn't have felt cornered, wouldn't have felt so alone, so hopeless, and wouldn't have given them such a lesson.

Perhaps not.

Ah, look at me carrying on as if I actually care. Forgive me.

Whatever the motivation, Vincent took it with him on that calm cloudless morning.

NAILED IT

It was a Friday.

He woke early, dressed in black (of course), smoked a massive dose of meth, and beat his foster parents to death with a framing hammer.

He stole a pick-up truck and blitzkrieg'd his way through the unsuspecting hive of conformity. Past the homogenized homes with dewy front yards, past the broken patterns of kids walking to school, past the darkened windows of the church.

The truck squealed and belched fire and black smog in its wake. Vincent punished that rusted hunk of metal, taking out street signs, colliding with parked cars, terrorizing pedestrians, and sending the engine into snarling distress.

With music pumping from the speakers, heralding his mayhem, he pushed the vehicle to its limit, driving hard and fast, until finally crashing through the glass entry of the high school.

Security cameras show he popped the trunk, retrieved a shotgun and stun-grenades, and marched through the fractured doors with his weapon raised, ready to fire.

He used the stun-grenades to scatter the cattle of students to clear his path and hunt his prey.

He killed the school security guard with a blast to the chest when the silly sod tried spraying him with mace. My father didn't even pause. He moved through the corridors terrifying students and teachers alike.

He marched past his locker, covered in a bully's graffiti, *DIE FAG*, and burst into the counselor's office with a hillbilly "yee-haw" and fired two shots killing the star quarterback and school counselor in mid-coitus.

Now you see why the rumors dispersed the way they did. I bet the CSI folks had a good laugh with this one.

The steroid enriched body of the quarterback with his polyester sweatpants slung down around his hairy ankles, his lumpy body slumped between the varicose veined legs of the pear-shaped, pointy faced school counselor, both with their brains blown all over the walls and decrepit vinyl sofa.

I've seen the crime scene photos and there looks to be a divine light emanating from the ghastly scene.

If Caravaggio were a photographer that's what he'd shoot.

A few hours later the police found the body of what once was Vincent hanging in the music room with a note pinned to his shirt that read, *I win.*

News personalities would speculate that Vincent's drug use had pushed him to this madness.

Daytime talk-show psychoanalysts would say he'd been bullied to a point of no return.

But Vincent is the only one who knows the truth and he isn't saying anything anymore.

Soon after, Cassandra had a nervous breakdown. Not about this of course. No, her problem was she had started *'to show'* and no one would give her dope with a baby in her belly.

She tried to get an abortion but at seven months no clinic would take her. And with Vincent rotting in the ground, there was no one evil enough to turn to.

So, in pure selfish desperation, she crouched behind a dumpster and guzzled a bottle of caster oil because she heard it induces labor. *It does.*

Half an hour of torturous spasms, Cassandra puked, and shat me out in an alley behind a dive bar. I was carefully tucked away while she went on the hunt for a fix. She was busted twenty minutes later trying to score blow and oxy's from an undercover cop.

He saw the blood, she spilled her guts, and they found me in the dumpster, wrapped in her varsity tennis jacket.

Cassandra was shipped off to a faith-based juvenile mental health facility where she lasted three weeks before running away. She was found eight months later in New Jersey.

Not to be droll, but Cassandra's fate is predictable. She died punctured, with a dick in her ass and a needle in her arm.

Her parents had her cremated and sealed away someplace. *Probably the rubbish bin.*

I spent the first six weeks of my life detoxing in the Intensive Care Unit. Once I reached a healthy weight and all the opiates were gone from my system, I was turned over to the cold, unloving arms of Cassandra's parents.

The shame of my birth was too much of a stain on their conservative social standing for me to remain in their household.

So, with the help of their Minister, beloved Granny and Pepaw sold me to an unscrupulous group of corporate ogres that knew how to handle *things like this* discreetly.

I doubt Cassandra's parents ever knew where I'd be sent or who I'd end up with.

They just wanted all this to go away. *And for them, it did.*

FORGING THE DEVIL

I was taken by private cargo plane
in an animal crate to a quiet suburb outside of
Plano, Texas.

On the outside, a normal house with a
manicured lawn and hedges, but inside, a
nefarious factory was working furiously night
and day.

I was given medical exams to check the
flexibility of my limbs, injected with a variety of

antibiotics, steroids, and vitamin supplements, subjected to hours and hours of amateur internet porn, and forced to endure certain devices that improved my primary instinct for suckling.

You will forgive me if I neglect to include the lewd details of their intentions.

It shouldn't be difficult to discern the objectives of professional flesh peddlers.

But I digress.

I remember there were others like me, similar in age and size. We weren't allowed to play together, as infants might, and we slept in tiny boxes that doubled as coffins.

Once I had achieved a certain level of physical strength and stamina, I was passed around, from club to club, in 22 states, where wealthy men fed their lecherous pleasures on the purity of young blood.

Eventually, I was pawned off to a rather violent and merciless brokerage called The Dominion made infamous by the high turnover rate of their drudges.

They had no rules or regulations. Whatever someone was willing to pay for, they got. I suppose my high pain tolerance and ability to mend quickly made me a perfect match for these devils.

Their command center was at the Golden Eagle Hotel, a ramshackle architectural fossil snug deep as thorns in the skid row district of downtown Los Angeles.

The clients paid for seclusion, not elegance. The Dominion used an entire floor. Each ratty room had a different client and different girl.

Nothing was out of bounds.

THE HARVEST

My handlers were called Cain & Smith.

Cain was a large Nigerian imbecile with a severe overbite. He dressed like a moron, always wearing a red Moroccan fez with a gold tassel and a giant gold chain. He cracked his knuckles compulsively. He enjoyed afternoon bouts with the youngest of us, "snacks" he called it.

Smith was a skinny balding Serbian imp

that took comb-over to new extremes. Aside from his paper cut smile, his large eyes dominated his crooked face.

His left eye was black as coal and his right was white and shiny as a hardboiled egg. He never touched us sexually. He was a voyeur. He liked to watch, which explains the plethora of security cameras in every room.

Cain and Smith worked for a group called The Dominion. And they were model employees and perfected the vicious brutality championed by their employers.

Smith was weak, but made up for it by being extremely demented and creative.

Cain was given the dirty work. If we

disobeyed, Cain was the lawgiver.

I was strong and sturdy, so they gave me to their most violent clientele. I spent months in and out of a body cast to reset broken hips. While I healed, I was kept offsite at a little clinic in Korea-town.

The nurses were Croatian, and all wore handwritten sticky-labels on their white polyester suits with stripper names like Destiny, Daisy, Crystal, and Cherry.

I was locked in a back room near a window. There were others there too. We were kept in plastic bins with a drainage hole that doubled as coffins.

I remember the sounds of their suffering

73

but couldn't see them over the sides of the small tubs.

The nurses only checked on us once a day, maybe twice if we were lucky. They rarely remembered to administer pain meds, or feed us, and would stifle our urgent cries by placing the corner of a dirty washcloth in our mouths that had been soaked in vodka. At least the booze numbed the pain and we could sleep from time to time.

As horrifying as this was, I must admit I hold a degree of gratitude for this experience for it led me to my eventual emancipation. Allow me to explain.

The cruelest nurse that attended me used the name "Charity". The irony wasn't lost on me. In my minds-eye I can still see the copper hair haloing her slender face, those boney fingers and deer-brown eyes gloating over me as she ashed her cigarette into my wounds. If I screamed, she would smother me until I passed out.

The day of my reckoning sprang out of instinct. She was fishing around in my mouth trying to put the washcloth in, but I struggled and bit the fuck out of her finger. My teeth clicked on bone. She screamed like a cat in a frying pan.

And then it happened.

An empowering thought planted itself firmly inside my mind. I'd never before fought back but now I understood I could hurt them. I realized just how weak and meaningless these creatures were. I could take whatever they dished out and more. But they couldn't. *They wouldn't.*

RESURRECTION

I remember the day my fear died.

I remember the day I didn't cry anymore. I remember when I vowed, regardless of penalty, to never serve The Dominion again.

When I finally healed, I was given back to my handlers, Cain and Smith. As soon as they saw me, they knew I was different. I was no longer theirs.

I killed my first meature when I was seven, a Saudi oil tycoon. I crept to the bed as he slept and carved up his genitals with the straight razor from his shaving kit. *He bled-out screaming like a pig.*

I killed my second, a Russian mob boss, by electrocution. I found a taser in his bag. I used a rubber band to compress the on-switch and dropped the 900k-volt gadget between his legs in the bath.

The water crackled and his body convulsed like a sliver of bacon on a hot pan. The smell of electri-fried hair and musk cologne tainted that room evermore. To this day I can't eat bacon.

My third was a red-blooded, middle-aged, heroin addict oil company Executive. As requested, I injected a sweet dose of expensive smack into a large penal vein.

He shoved me to the corner, "Wait for me there, honey pot. I'll be out of this soon and we can get back to...." he slipped into slobbering blackness.

I stood from the floor, empty syringe in hand, and walked to him. I pulled back the plunger and pumped a dose of air into the tracked, scabbed shaft of his crooked penis.

The air bubble reached his heart immediately. His body jolted upright and fell hard to the carpet.

I stabbed the needle into his eardrum and

sat on the floor next to his bloated corpse. I smiled at the security camera and waited.

As I waited, I stared at my many bruises, the polychrome hues from green to purple to black. Green meant healing. Black was new. I had very little green on me.

It wasn't long before I heard footsteps beating down the hall towards my room.

They punished me quite often and rather cruelly for my newfound sedition.

But, oh gentle reader, *it was worth it.*

They broke my arm for the Saudi, they starved me in a crate for the Russian, and broke my jaw for laughing (like a lunatic) after 100 or so lashes from the belt for various other discretions.

But the Oil Company Executive was an important client for them and his death impacted their cash and their security.

Smith and Cain burst into the room. Cain screamed, "Stupid fucking bitch!" and punched me in the head.

"Again you do this? Someone will come looking for him!"

Smith spit on me, "Fuck that. You know how much money we just lost?"

This act of rebellion wouldn't be forgiven. Smith deemed me unsalvageable, "She's fucking broken, man. I'm done with her."

He ordered Cain to give me a final reprimand. "Get rid of the bitch. Fucking kill her."

Cain grunted and obliged in excess. He started beating me. *Mercilessly.*

I assumed the usual position on my side, covering my head with one hand and placing the other between my legs.

He kicked and punched. I started blacking out but could hear Smith's phone ringing. *Text message.*

He snarled at Cain, "Hold up. We just found a taker."

Cain wheezed, "Who?"

Smith laughed, "Fucking Eckhart wants her,"

Cain grimaced, "Shit, man. Really? Fuck. I almost feel sorry for her."

They both erupted into laughter and I slipped into the dark swamp of my subconscious.

ECKHART

Hours later, days maybe, I can't be sure, but I woke bloody and sore on a dirty kitchen floor that was covered in grease and rotten bits of food. I could hear the roaches scurring across counter tops cluttered with crusty crockery.

Except for mold the walls were bare. The place stunk of old piss and decay.

I could see a shadowy hulk of a man

seated on a metal folding chair leaning over a small table typing furiously on his computer with a single finger from each hand. He mumbled every word he typed.

Though this room was empty, the remaining rooms were packed floor to ceiling with newspapers, magazines, books, water jugs, medical supplies, knives, batteries, packaged food, guns, flashlights, match boxes, Bibles, small ordinances and boxes and boxes of small arms ammunition.

This hoarder's paradise belonged to the man seated at the computer. You wouldn't know it, but behind those thick glasses smeared with food and sweat, beneath the scruffy beard, and yellowed smile was once a ruggedly handsome man thought to be a genius. But now, here sits a man swallowed by his derangements.

This was Eckhart, *my savior.*

He kept me drugged for the first few weeks. Taking care to nurse my wounds and infections in the basement of his shitty house. I wasn't the first.

There were signs that others had been there before me. Ugly graffiti, prayers and etchings of forget-me-nots were left behind by frightened souls who must have accepted their terrible fate.

Eckhart believed God ordained him for a special mission. He believed the end of the world was coming and he was chosen to save the human race by reinventing it in his image.

God had told him that if he did things just right, he would become a god of this world once the rapture came.

Apparently the old God was ready for retirement and Eckhart was to take his place.

He was told to find and shape the new "Eve" - a feeding, fucking, subjugated baby-machine that would repopulate the world with his seed.

He used The Dominion to find the girls. So far, none of them were worthy. He was eager to see if I would be the one.

He fed me once a day - a grueling slop of

blended amino acids, vitamin supplements, and assorted meats he carved from road kill.

Physical violence wasn't the only way he tried subjugating me, mental and emotional abuse rallied from his mind like a sewer overflowing with filth.

He covered all the mirrors in his house and removed anything reflective from the basement.

"You're too ugly," he would say, "you're lucky you have me. No one else would EVER be able to love you like I do."

Though these remarks were meant to injure me into submission, I realized it was his damaged esteem he was protecting.

I don't think his ego could stand to lose another member of the Eve Project. That's what he called it. He had a lot of projects.

Though he owned me, part of him needed me to need him, to agree with him, to see his truth. And if aggression didn't work, fear was administered.

He forced me to wear a gas mask and never take it off. He said we had to stay prepared, that the end could happen at any moment.

I know he was conditioning me, but I also believe he thought this *to be true.*

He would sometimes stand for hours just

staring at the ceiling as if in trance. He would have visions of angels and demons waging war in the skies above us.

He said we'd wait until my wounds healed before we'd have *"holy intercourse"*. Eckhart wanted to train me first.

He taught me to cook his favorite meals and the proper way "a lady" serves the man of the house. And he beat me regularly just to keep the demons from clinging to my soul.

He used an electrical cable in hopes of whipping the evil out of me, and then forced me to soak in an ice-baths for hours at a time.

Though his treatment of me was cruel and laborious, it was a welcome change from the barbarous living at The Dominion.

Besides, he'd shown me a small kindness in allowing my bruises to heal before he touched me.

I'd forgotten what my skin looked like without them. In some strange way, I felt indebted to him for this.

He was mentally divergent but I found some of his theories interesting and entertaining. I suppose I wasn't engineered to withstand bullshit for too long. In fact, I think have an allergy to it.

As these proclamations tend to do, one day it just came to me. A simple thought as one might have when deciding to take a walk.

Tomorrow, I would kill Eckhart.

And so, the next morning I made his favorite breakfast: scrambled eggs mixed with boiled bologna and pickle slices covered in ketchup.

This time, however, I added my own spice, a lethal poison from Eckhart's personal stash.

A few bites in and he fell to the floor in a violent, frothy seizure and squeaked out a squeal that, at the time, I found quite humorous. I know he couldn't see my face beneath my gas mask, but I promise you, my smile was ear-to-ear.

I sat with his lump of a body for a day or so not really knowing what to do next.

I accidentally saw my reflection in an uncovered window. My hair sprouted from the gas mask in random patches like weeds in the cracks of a sidewalk.

I was too afraid to remove it. The months of conditioning had momentarily succeeded.

What if he was right? What if I really was that repulsive?

For now, I'd leave it be and felt the warmth of safety wash over me.

My mind was clear now. I knew my mission. I was to kill as many of them as I could in the most treacherous and painful ways imaginable for as long as I was alive.

Without thinking, I took his knife and carefully removed his face and fingers. I burned them in the sink.

I commandeered his emergency rations, medical supplies, and, of course, plenty of ammo.

I waited until dark and crept out after Cain and Smith. I was determined to bring down The Dominion or die trying.

I was fortunate that at that late hour, buses in Los Angeles are always filled with freaks and misfits.

There I was, nine years old, sitting at the back of the bus wrapped in a hospital gown, carrying an old doctor's kit packed with guns and supplies, wearing a World War Two era gas mask, and no one acted surprised or alarmed.

The passing landscape of lights and street lamps reflected in the green glass of my eyeholes.

By the time the bus reached downtown, I was ready. I stepped off and snuck around to the back of the Golden Eagle hotel.

I slipped in through a broken window and prepared for the hunt in the stairwell. Eckhart had prepared the bag long ago. Inside were assorted knives with holsters, two .45 automatic handguns, extra rounds, flash grenades, and small latex balloons filled with homemade napalm.

I slung the bag around my shoulders, and, with both fists gripping a gun, marched through the hotel firing at anyone who ran.

This was a busy hour for The Dominion and most every room was full.

I walked casually down the corridor, opened doors and tossed in the napalm balloons at random.

People ran screaming, consumed by chemical fire, past me in the hallway.

I emptied the first clip and slid in a new one just in time to gun down a Minister who was trying to escape with a young boy in tow.

I'd reached the final corner of the crooked hallway but Cain and Smith were nowhere to be found.

I popped open the final door and inside was a bulging mountain of a man desperately trying to pull his pants up.

He swiveled to me, shirtless and masses of black hair sprouted from his fleshy limbs like leggy spiders.

He was balding on top but his dark eyes were framed by a thick uni-brow.

He screamed something in Slovakian and spittle stuck in his thick moustache like morning dew.

In the corner, trembling naked was a girl about my age. She was still covered in the relics of the rape.

My mind drifted momentarily to the sound of my breath inside the gas mask.

The man-mountain moved toward me and I shot him once in the chest. Blood vomited from his mouth. I must've hit a lung.

He fell over, choking and spitting.

I dropped the bag to the floor and motioned for the girl to flee. She did.

I retrieved a butcher's saw from the bag

and cut off his head then dropped it in the toilet.

Just then, Cain and Smith burst into the room led by the girl I just saved.

This confused me momentarily and gave Cain the time to rush me and shove me to the floor. I just had time to shoot him in the thigh before he struck me.

I remember his size 11 boot coming fast at my face, the impact, and then nothingness.

My consciousness resurfaced just as he dropped me from the third story window. The frigid winds rushing past me as I plummeted into the alley. The dumpster again. But this time I landed next to it, hard on the pavement.

Smith blew me a kiss and closed the window leaving me to die in the rain.

Lucky for me I had another savior. If not for the man I know only as The Founder, I would have died that night on the cold concrete.

This is where the story coils into something profound and has proven to me my life is purposeful.

You see, The Founder was on his way to kill the man I did.

FOUNDING FATHER

Apparently my broken body

just missed him as it crashed to the street. He'd
heard the wind whipping and pulled his assault
rifle out of the way just as I whizzed by.

You may or may not believe in this sort
of thing but some might say the universe was
conspiring in my favor.

The Founder was a mercenary. Political
assassination and faux terrorist attacks were his

specialty, but, occasionally, he did smaller jobs, just for fun. Lucky for me, the human shit-bag that I beheaded had a nosey wife who found out about his lecherous child-raping hobbies and hired The Founder to grease him.

Kismet is a motherfucker.

So, there I was, broken and bleeding to death, about to expire, when The Founder pulled my limp body into the basement of the Golden Eagle Hotel.

He secured me near the boiler to keep me warm and then ascended the fire stairs to the third floor.

He found Cain and Smith bitching about having to clean all these bodies and finding replacement girls. Smith groaned, "This is fucked up, man. If The Board hears about this, we are dead fucking meat. We have to hide these goddamn bodies."

Cain grumbled back, "This one already fucking stinks. And where are we going to find another batch of girls?"

The Founder used the barrel of his HK416 assault rifle to crack the door and then, without warning, massacred those swine.

There really is nothing so beautiful as the violent opera of a machine gun with a silencer.

The orange conical fire hissing from the barrel of the gun, the hollow thuds of the bullets ripping through flesh, the tinny resonance of the shells raining to the floor. Blood and gore spraying the walls like a demented Jackson Pollack creation.

The Founder was truly an artist. He shot Cain through the mouth and prick, and Smith in both eyes, and then walked room-to-room exterminating the paying vermin and their tiny slaves.

I remember regaining consciousness for a moment to see him carrying a heavy barrel of gasoline up the stairs.

And later, waking to see the empty gasoline barrel lying on its side next to me. Then the sound and smell of fire, and the screams of those he trapped inside.

He later explained he thought sending the girls to heaven was a better end than the eventual end of meth addiction and prostitution destiny logically had in store for them.

He wrapped me in a blanket and carried me to his van. I was placed in the back and told to remain quiet. I did.

I must have passed out again because I don't remember the ride. I can only recall The Founder gently placing me on a gurney and this foreign sense of safety washing over me.

I could see him better now. No helmet, no combat gear. Shaved head, pencil-thin mustache, grey eyes. He spoke softly, "Welcome, my dear, to Armana".

THE BUTCHER, THE BAKER

Kill Log: 214323

She's late. I hate it when they're late. I've been sitting inside this room all afternoon inhaling a nauseating mélange of vanilla extract and cat piss.

She's a hoarder, this one, and she bakes. Every Sunday, she totes a bundle of cherry cupcakes, chocolate chunk cookies and gingerbread men with red-icing eyes to the homeless shelter.

Little do these homeless scumbags know that their sugary sweeties are laced with a microscopic gristle of mold, skin flakes, cat hair, and rat shit.

She's a despicable creature, this one. Her home is bloated with clutter. Walls within walls, I have been hiding in a labyrinth of rubbish for two days and she's never suspected a thing.

She eats half of what she bakes and her body looks to be over-inflated and ready to burst. Her thighs rub together when she walks and make a sound like sandpaper on wood. Despite having mounds and mounds of new and used clothing, she wears only three outfits from her crowded closet.

She hasn't washed her dun-colored hair in probably a decade. It smells like it at least. She paints her face like a doll. Giant circles of rouge stain her jowls, her eyelids are thick with a heavy coat of sky blue eye shadow, and she applies her ruby red lipstick like a hobo clown.

Aside from the towers of trash, every corner and cove is covered in cat shit. She collects them. Cats. Not shit. Well, maybe she does. But definitely cats. I've counted twenty-two so far but I've heard others, howling in the parapets, lost and hungry.

Oh, I have such a beautiful plan for this one but I'm growing desperately impatient. The stench is overwhelming and starting to cling.

And just when I feel like I can't take it

anymore, the front door finally creaks open. Her shrill voice streaks through the dwelling. She greets the cluster of cats rushing the door.

"Hellooo babies. Mama is home. Did you miss me? Did you miss Mama? Oh, I missed you."

I want to burn this place to the ground.

From the other room I hear, "Socks! You bully-boo! Stop picking on your brother. Play nice" followed by a labored grunting as she pushes her way through the narrow gaps in the piles of rotting junk.

"Come with Mommy," she wheezes, "let's make din-din. Come with Mommy".

The cats follow meowing and whipping their tails like fly-fishermen.

She wobbles into the crowded kitchen with twenty-two half-starved cats shuffling around her feet. She opens a can of generic cat food and the slop slides from the tin without losing its shape.

It glops to the crusty floor and the cats converge. It's gone in matter of seconds.

She inches into the TV room with a bag of jumbo marshmallows and a bottle of chocolate syrup.

She sits on the only bit of furniture that is unencumbered, a stained green recliner, and switches on the TV.

A nature show pops on and she sinks into the chair like a pillowy corpse.

I can see her from my hiding place. Her dead eyes reflecting the switching colors from the aged screen, sloppy mouth agape and stained with color.

The TV host narrates in a monotone cadence as a group of ugly birds gulp down sea turtle eggs.

She squirts syrup into her mouth and takes a greedy bite from a monstrous marshmallow.

She is unknowingly imitating the mouth movements of the birds chomping through the shells.

I smell warm piss. She's wetting herself in the chair. The stains on the cushion tell me she does this quite often. *Fucking lazy flotsam.* I've seen quite enough. I rise slowly in front of her, pushing through the mound of litter like a demon rising from the mud. Her mouth falls open, chewed pieces of marshmallow stick in her coffee colored teeth. I must look like a living shadow to her in this black nylon suit. It does not reflect light and has no seams.

She doesn't scream. She doesn't move.

I raise my arms like a crucifixion and she sinks further into the filth of the recliner.

I sense she is about to speak so I quiet her with a hard boot to the stomach. She eeks a scream as the air explodes from her lungs and her body slumps to the cushions edge.

I shove her back into the chair and ram fistfuls of marshmallows down her throat.

She retches and struggles for air. I shove them all into her mouth and pack them tight. I empty the bottle of syrup over the top and shove the mass into her throat.

She's choking and lurching.

I tie the empty marshmallow bag over her head. Her eyes bulge and her face burns purple.

The smell of her unwashed hair and scabby body is too much. I spin away and bring out my PPK with the extra quiet silencer. I fire six shots, two in the chest, one in the stomach, one in the neck, and two in the head.

Her body folds like a dead spider.

The smell of gunpowder eases the odor of this place. The cats should feed well for a week, maybe two. Some were already circling her carcass before I left. A few more were licking the blood and chocolate syrup from her face.

I cut out her tongue for my collection, shut off the TV, and steal away into the night.

Destination: Haz-Mat shower

"The Lord is a man of war.

The Lord is his name."

- Exodus 15:3

PUPA

Armana was his center of operations and was an abandoned nuclear plant with two massive cooling towers that would incite a primitive fear in passersby as if they were staring at a dormant volcano or the petrified corpse of a fallen giant.

He said he purchased the land using one of his offshore companies (arms dealing) and hired the security agency he owned to look after the place.

He assured me, "We'll be safe here."

I was consigned to the lower level of the facility. I slept in the old HazMat chamber because it had a shower. The rest of the rooms and chambers were either locked or empty.

The Founder took great care in my rehabilitation. After only a few months, I was walking again. He gave me coveralls and a pair of boots that still had the old atomic insignia on it.

He cut my hair to look like a boy and called me Hunter just in case anyone ever saw us together on any training missions.

The Founder was deadly but The Dominion was powerful. He knew they might try to find us and wanted to protect me from slipping back into their filthy clutches.

Camouflage was our first line of defense. Our second line was guns. *Lots and lots of guns.*

We used the underground tunnels of Armana to set up a firing range.

My first pistol was a Walther PPK. Black on black. A "pocket pistol", he called it. I cherished it. It was loud and terrifying. Hitler used one to commit suicide. *Fine gun, the PPK.*

My second was a Winchester repeater rifle. The recoil was smooth and it fired like a dream. I could pick off six targets in row without missing a single shot, even if they scattered.

A 12 gauge Mossberg was next. The power of that gun is indescribable. I instantly fell in love with it. I was surgical with my aim and could vivisect a target at fifty feet.

Next was sniper training. "Alley kills" he called them. We'd sneak off in the night and perch atop an old meatpacking plant, picking off hungry scavengers feeding from the filth and excess of this world.

Drug dealers, pimps, users, johns, and the occasional hooker - headshots - nothing else was acceptable.

We used paraffin bullets that dissolved upon impact. (The cops never solved those murders. I guess they can now. You're welcome, pigs.)

The Founder enjoyed bestowing his extensive mastery of armaments upon me: 9mm and .45 caliber automatics, submachine guns, automatic shotguns, assault rifles, and explosives.

But my favorite was a specialized handheld Gatling gun that could cut an enemy to pieces in a matter of seconds. It was larger than an uzi but smaller and lighter than the HK.

He taught me the proper way to use a blade in close combat: how to grip a knife, where to stab, where to slice, and how to evade the blade of an opponent.

As an award for my achievements, he

gave me a beautiful hunting knife with a black blade. It can cut flesh with the slightest effort.

The dark blade was serrated and the handle had finger holes that doubled as brass knuckles. I have found this to be a very useful instrument. (If you hit the heart just right you can hear it pop like a leather balloon)

I was given daily intelligence tests and forced to read books on survival tactics, military strategy and covert ops. On Sundays he would read a different chapter from a different ideology.

I think he sensed a level of barrenness in me that would never fully comprehend mercy or regret.

So he tried, abortively, to teach me selective compassion through the philosophies and religious texts from various teachers and cultures. It didn't work. He couldn't divert my nature.

All he could do was hope to nurture my destructive instincts toward his confusing and contradictory ethical code.

"We kill the weak," he'd bellow, "and conquer the wicked. We must eradicate them before they infect us with their turpitude."

I'm not sure where his work as a mercenary or the arms dealing fell into his moral code, but he was unwavering. "We use the devil's money to do the Lord's work," he'd say and wink at me.

His ethos has stayed with me, however, and I am happy to have had a mentor like him. I do the big jobs for the greater good, but the small ones are just for me.

He'd sometimes go away to help overthrow a dictator, murder a warlord, install a military junta, or whatever it is that mercenaries do, and I'd be left alone, locked in the lower levels of Armana to fend for myself.

Sometimes I was only given a few days worth of rations and I had to extend them for months. I was expected to keep up my weapons training and literary studies. *And I did.*

The isolation didn't bother me. After years of uninvited company, it was nice to be alone and unencumbered.

One day I found an unlocked exhaust portal that was big enough for me to wriggle through. It led to a network of pipes and drains and porticos that gave access to the rest of the facility.

The Founder always said there were others in the upper levels of Armana, employees of his security firm, but I spent months and months exploring the dilapidated facility and never once saw another living soul.

(I suppose it says something about the type of world your species has created when my one and only moral compass was a professional killer and serial liar. But I digress.)

He'd always return unannounced and try to surprise me with a sneak attack.

The fisticuffs would be real, but we'd both stop short of using whatever weapon was close at hand.

At first, I didn't stand a chance. He'd catch me asleep and use a nylon chord to strangle me until I either blacked out or wiggled free.

Or he 'd find me walking aimlessly in the corridors of lower Armana and blast me with a beanbag round from his shotgun.

Sometimes he'd leap from the shadows and we'd fight until I submitted. The only time I ever beat him at this game was thanks to my secret portal.

I was just about to slink from the exhaust door when I heard him coming down the hall. I waited until he passed, then quietly slid into the corridor and attacked him from behind. I jump-kicked him in the back and choked him until he yielded.

He never figured out how I did it and *I never told.*

When I reached puberty, he showed me a video on the Internet about menstrual cycles. When it was over he stood at the door with his back to me.

"You'll be a woman very soon," he said, "and I'll come calling. It's nothing emotional.

It's a natural act. I won't force you but I expect you to be receptive."

Expectations are dangerous.

This was a command I couldn't follow. Yes, he had been a grand benefactor, truly, my savior. But if history has taught us anything it is that all movements need a martyr.

Martyrs die.

It was just before midnight when it happened. I was lying in my HazMat chamber staring at the shadows the red emergency bulb casts on my ceiling when I heard soft steps approaching.

I turned my back to the door and

pretended to sleep. The Founder stepped inside.

I was calm and showed no signs of detection. He removed his robe and folded it neatly on the table. He placed his master key next to it and exhaled slowly.

He seemed nervous. The kind of apprehension someone might have trying to sneak past a sleeping crocodile.

In a flash, he was behind me, naked, beneath my blanket. He reached for my shoulder and pulled me close. His heart was racing and his breathing became rapid.

"I'm only doing to you what nature compels me to do," he whispered. "Don't fight and I won't hurt you."

I turned to him. I kept my body soft and slack. He wouldn't look at me. I nodded a quiet *yes.*

He slid his hands between my legs and removed my panties. He pressed his weight on me. I feigned submission. He reached down to propel himself into me *but I penetrated first.*

My knife punctured his throat and blood exploded from the wound. He fell off me and I sent my blade into his lung and again into his liver. Just as he taught me.

Blood gushed into his airway, he gurgled, drowning. I penetrated his stomach and swung around to his kidneys. His body opened up like a busted tin of biscuits. Just as he taught me.

I stabbed him again and again. He didn't utter a word of protest. He didn't fight back. He didn't look angry or confused.

He just died.

I removed his head and hands and placed them in a cooling locker. I wrapped his body in a blanket and drug it to the furnace. He was ash in a matter of minutes.

I recovered his card key and entered Upper Armana. Here, I will continue my studies and training.

Here, I will blossom and destroy.

THE END...?

ONE MORE THING

I've been on a bit of a hiatus from
these reports (I'm sure you've noticed) and for
that I do apologize. I know how much you
adore observing doom. But it's not without
regret, I assure you, gentle reader. It's just that
I've been so busy carving up more and more
meatures that I don't have time to write.

It seems there's been a population
explosion thanks to boner pills (parlance) and
fertility drugs, and the expansion of political

139

bozos with no moral filter, not to mention the availability and cultural acceptance of booze and designer drugs. Your species is breeding like rats. Though, I don't mean to insults rats when I compare the two. But you understand.

It's difficult for me to take time to transfer my journals and diaries and kill logs while I'm busy butchering these dregs.

There's so much evil. It's so much fun. Besides, when the barbarian becomes king or when the warrior becomes queen, when seated upon a throne of ash and bone, seated as a conqueror, seated among the ruins and the wreckage, all one can do (I can assure you) is either sink into shadow or pursue another battle. Lucky for me, nemesis abound.

For example, there was that has-been, wanna-be (parlance) singer from some forgotten band who was raping young fans, I poured acid in his eyes and ran electrical wires into his urethra. Then I carved him up and fed him to feral dogs.

There was the CEO who posted photos of her *safari kills* online. Such a pathetic coward. She paid a kings ransom to shoot elephants and lions chained in their cages. Where's the sport in that? She's no hunter. I tracked and captured her, then I cut off her feet and dropped in her the bear pit at the zoo. They tried to eat her, but the meat was too gamey for their tastes I think. They did seem to like the gallon of honey I made her ingest earlier in the day. They opened her guts up pretty quick. The birds did the rest.

I tarred and feathered and then anally electrocuted a child rapist until flames shot out his eyes. That was fun.

And there was the man who drowned his son in the bath for crying too much. Lucky for me he lived in an isolated area. I removed his manhood with a dull butter knife (disgusting work) and fed it to him through a funnel with stewed carrots and onions. After dinner, I broke the bones in his hands, knocked out his teeth (one by one) with a cobblers hammer, and then used his wife's iron (on the cotton setting) to roast his back. The smell was atrocious. He fainted a few times. A couple of ice baths took care of that. But then I got bored with all the "please, stop" and the "my father's got money" and "I'll do anything you want" bullshit. So, I disemboweled him, first pulling the intestines out with a crank and wheel device of my own design, so messy but very effective, then spooned out his liver, and finally his plucked out his heart. Then I ran what was left of him into a meat grinder and fed him to the fish at a salmon farm. Some of you might've enjoyed him, second hand of course, at your local sushi bars or maybe when you ordered the smoked salmon and vegetables from the 'healthy heart' menu. Maybe that's what they mean when they say you are what you eat.

So, you see, dear reader, I'm not gone, not really, I'm just simply encumbered. But fret not, I do plan on taking some time for myself in the near future when I can relive all these beautiful moments with you in these transcriptions and release more salvations to the world. If you're lucky, I'll include visuals.

Until then, you have my undying devotion. None shall sleep. I'll visit you in your dreams. And to any police organizations that might be reading this, don't even attempt to find any evidence on how to locate me from these writings. I'm smarter than you and you know it. Trust me, when I'm ready, I'll find YOU.

Lovingly,
Hydra Moonlight

AFTERWORD

My lawyers say I must include this after bit. This book is art. It's fantasy. It's not meant to condone or incite violence or murder. I don't. If you know anything about my writing or me then you already know what this is.
It's fun.

Love & stitches,
Otep

Otep Shamaya is an artist, activist, author, a GLAAD nominee, cultural arsonist, & intellectual loudmouth with a fearless passion for justice & the preservation of the arts. This is her first book of fiction.

Live to Defy.

Centaurs Breed Publishing

For information about this publication contact:
you@artsaves.me or online at www.artsaves.me

Also by Otep Shamaya

- Caught Screaming
- The Myth
- Quiet Lightning on the Noisy Mountain
- The Sugar Shack
- New Word Order
- Gnaw Bone

Find them online at:

- www. lulu.com/spotlight/otepsaves

Find Otep Shamaya online at:

- www.artsaves.com
- www.twitter.com/otepofficial
- www.facebook.com/otepofficial
- www.instagram.com/otep_shamaya

NONE SHALL SLEEP

Written by Otep Shamaya

Copyright © OTEP SHAMAYA 2013

Cover design by Joey James

Artworxofjoeyjames@facebook.com

Centaurs Breed Publishing

For information about this publication contact:

you@artsaves.me or online at www.artsaves.me

NONE

SHALL

SLEEP